W9-ADO-292

Talia and the Very 'YUM' Kippur

LINDA ELOVITZ MARSHALL
ILLUSTRATED BY FRANCESCA ASSIRELLI

KAR-BEN PUBLISHING

For my grandchildren, the yummiest ever: Gabriel, Niomi, Julia Rose, Lyra, Avi, Talia, Leah, Noa, Baruch and those yet to come.
-L.E.M.

For my grandmothers, Wanda and Tita -F.A.

KAR-BEN PUBLISHING
A division of Lerner Publishing Group, Inc.
241 First Avenue North
Minneapolis, MN 55401 USA
1-800-4-KARBEN

Website address: www.karben.com

Main body text set in Adrianna Regular 15/20.
Typeface provided by Chank.

Library of Congress Cataloging-in-Publication Data

Marshall, Linda Elovitz.
Talia and the very YUM Kippur / by Linda Elovitz Marshall ; illustrated by Francesca Assirelli.
pages cm.
Summary: "Talia helps her grandmother prepare food for Yom Kippur, which she mishears as YUM Kippur, and learns the original meaning of break-fast"— Provided by publisher.
ISBN: 978-1-4677-5236-7 (lib. bdg. : alk. paper)
[1. Yom Kippur—Fiction. 2. Judaism—Customs and practices—Fiction. 3. Grandmothers—Fiction.]
I. Assirelli, Francesca, illustrator. II. Title.
PZ7.M35672453Tb 2015
[E]—dc23 2014028829

Manufactured in the United States of America
1 - VP - 7/15/15

Talia loved visiting her grandparents—especially in early fall, when their farm was full of wonderful smells and tastes.

"Talia, would you like to help prepare the Yom Kippur break-fast for tomorrow?" asked Grandma.

Wow! thought Talia. *A YUM Kippur breakfast!* She rubbed her tummy and answered, "Sure!"

Grandma put on her apron, took out a recipe, and said, "First, we'll make a kugel. We need three eggs. You know where to find them."

Talia went to the henhouse. *Yum!* she thought as she checked the hens' nests. *Delicious, fresh eggs.*

She carried the eggs—very, very carefully—back to her grandmother.

"Now we'll need some milk," said Grandma. "You can help Grandpa milk the cow."

Talia went to the barn with Grandpa. She held the bucket while Grandpa milked the cow. Then Grandpa showed Talia how to do the milking. A stream of milk squirted into the bucket. *Yum!* thought Talia. *Tasty, fresh milk.*

She carried the full bucket of milk—very, very carefully—back inside.

“Next we’ll need cottage cheese, noodles, raisins, sour cream, and sugar,” said Grandma.

Yum! thought Talia. *My favorites!* Talia searched the refrigerator and the pantry. She carried each ingredient—very, very carefully—to her grandmother.

They boiled the noodles and mixed in the raisins, sour cream, sugar, milk, and eggs. Then they put the kugel in the oven to bake.

For the rest of the day, Talia helped Grandma cook.
They made cookies and cakes, tuna salad and blintzes.

"Yum!" said Talia. "I can't wait to eat all this food." Grandma smiled. "We'll have to wait," she said. "It's for Yom Kippur—for the break-fast."

But the next morning, Grandma gave Talia fruit and cereal as usual. And the rest of the family didn't eat at all. Everyone except for Grandma and Talia dressed nicely and went to synagogue.

"Why didn't anyone eat?" Talia asked after the others had gone.

"It's a fast day," Grandma explained.

“Ohhhh,” said Talia, nodding. It must be a very fast day if no one had time for breakfast.

“But don’t worry,” said Grandma. “When everyone comes back, it will be time for the Yom Kippur break-fast.”

The house was very quiet that morning. Talia read her books and played with her dolls.

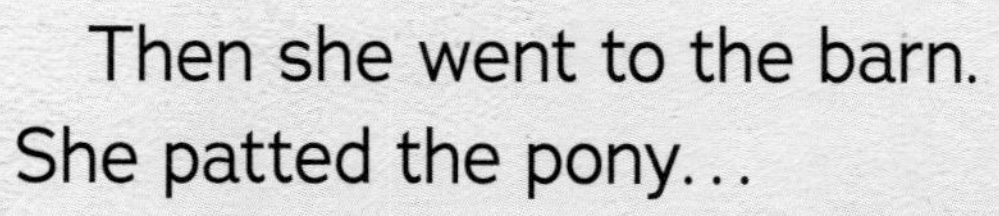

Then she went to the barn.
She patted the pony...

...played with the lambs...

...and cuddled the rabbits.

She looked at the leaves on the trees. They were turning beautiful fall colors. Every so often, one fell to the ground. It did not seem like a very fast day.

Talia went back inside. "When is the big breakfast?" she asked again.

"After sunset," said Grandma. "And it's a break-fast, not a breakfast."

Talia looked puzzled.

"It's *like* a big breakfast," Grandma explained, "but it comes at the end of a fast day."

"I don't think it's a fast day," Talia said. "I think it's a *slow* day."

Grandma laughed. "A fast day is a day when people don't eat," she told Talia. "On this holiday, Jews fast and pray and think about how to be better people."

"*That* doesn't sound very yummy," said Talia. "I thought today was *YUM* Kippur. I thought it was going to be delicious."

"It's *Yom* Kippur," said her grandmother, "but it *will* be delicious. Just wait. First, people spend time thinking about things they might have done better. If someone did something wrong or something that hurt someone's feelings, this is a time to ask for forgiveness."

Talia thought for a minute.

"Grandma," she said. "Remember that lamp my doll broke?"

Her grandmother nodded.

"It was me," Talia said. "Not my doll. I'm sorry I broke it. And I'm sorry I lied."

Her grandmother hugged her. *That* felt delicious.

"And I'm sorry I yelled at you then," her grandmother said. "Will you forgive me?"

They hugged again.

"*Yum!*" said Talia. "That feels really good."

Then Talia thought of something else. “Grandma,” she said, “I know we already made the food, but won’t you need help setting the table?”

Grandma smiled. “Yes, I will. Can you help me?”

“Of course!” said Talia.

So at sunset, she carried napkins, silverware, and dishes to the table. She set out plates of bagels and pitchers of juice. Grandma took the rest of the food out of the refrigerator. "Yum!" they said together when everything was ready.

Thanks to Talia and her grandmother, they all enjoyed a very sweet *YUM* Kippur.

YOM KIPPUR, also known as the Day of Atonement, comes ten days after Rosh Hashanah, the Jewish New Year. Adults and children over the age of bar/bat mitzvah fast, pray in the synagogue, and ask for forgiveness for things they have said or done in the previous year that may have hurt others. Family and friends gather to "break the fast" with a festive meal after sundown.

Talia's YUM Kippur Kugel

Ingredients for Kugel

1 package (12 oz.) wide flat egg noodles
2 Tbsp. butter, melted
16 oz. cottage cheese
16 oz. sour cream or yogurt
2 eggs, beaten
½ cup sugar
½ tsp. vanilla extract (optional)
1 tsp. cinnamon
1 cup raisins
¾ cup milk

Ingredients for topping

1 tsp. cinnamon
¼ cup sugar

Pre-heat oven to 350°. Butter a 9 x 12 baking dish. Boil the noodles, then drain, rinse and return them to the same pot for mixing. Add the rest of the ingredients to the noodles. Pour everything into the buttered 9 x12 baking dish. Mix together 1 tsp. cinnamon and ¼ cup sugar for the topping and sprinkle this on top of the kugel. Bake for ½ hour or until topping is browned and crisp. Kugel will feel firm but still soft when done. Cool and cut into squares. Serve as side dish or dessert.

Note: This recipe can be adjusted to taste. There is no such thing as a bad kugel!